Mavis the Bravest

NEST ♥ IS ♥ BEST

KNITTING for ANIMALS

For Lucinda, my 'Marge' . . . with love xxx – LF

To my sister Fiona, who found that a little bit of braveness changed everything. Then took up crochet as a new challenge – SW

SIMON & SCHUSTER
First published in Great Britain in 2023 by Simon & Schuster UK Ltd
1st Floor, 222 Gray's Inn Road, London WC1X 8HB

A CIP catalogue record for this book is available from
the British Library upon request

ISBN: 978-1-4711-9142-8 (HB)
ISBN: 978-1-4711-9143-5 (PB)
ISBN: 978-1-4711-9144-2 (eBook)

Printed in China
1 3 5 7 9 10 8 6 4 2

MIX
Paper | Supporting
responsible forestry
FSC® C144853
www.fsc.org

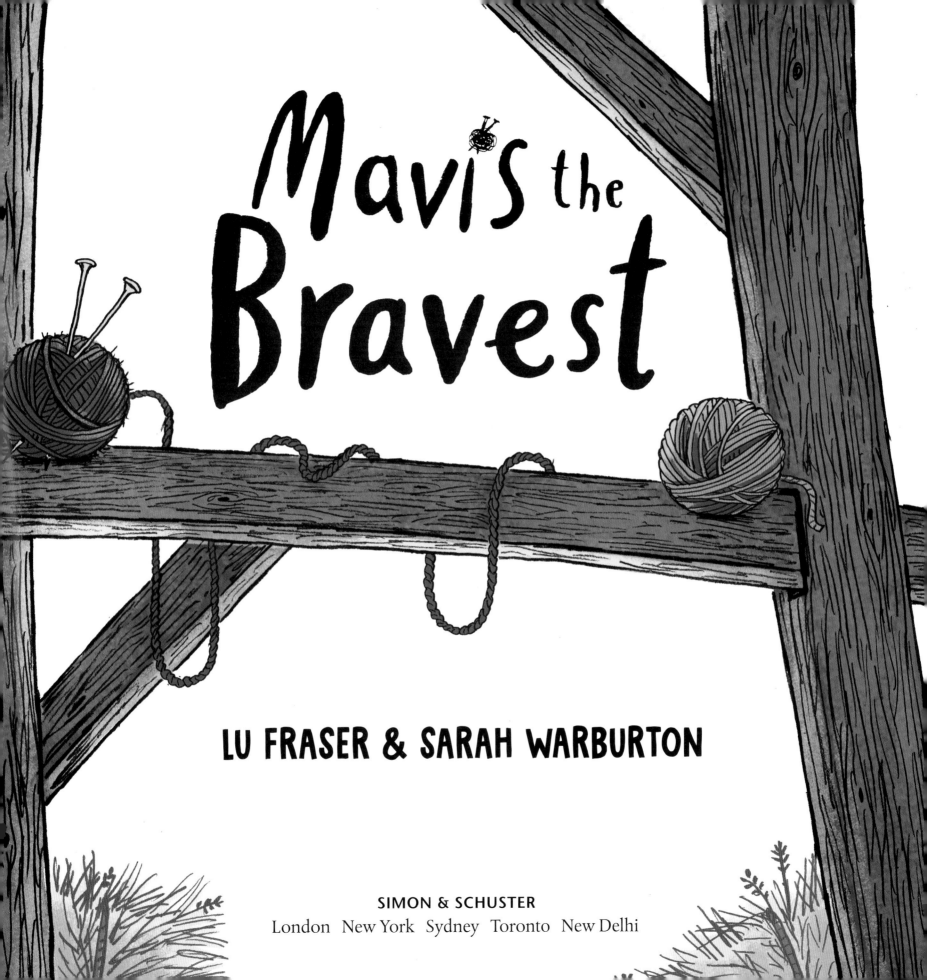

Mavis the Bravest

LU FRASER & SARAH WARBURTON

SIMON & SCHUSTER

London New York Sydney Toronto New Delhi

There's a slumbering hush in the barn on the hill.
As the stars twinkle down, all is calm, all is still.

No **mooing**, no **neighing**,

no **oinking**, no **quacking**,

Just rumbling snores …

and the faint sound of . . .
CLACKING!

For high in the rafters,
a small shape is sitting . . .

. . . It's Mavis the chicken,
click-clacking her KNITTING!

"I'm a bird," Mavis sighed, "who finds EVERYTHING scary,

Night-time . . .

and daytime . . .

and anything HAIRY!

LOUD things and FAST things

and anything WHIZZY!

And FLYING," she gulped, "makes me feel a bit dizzy!

So I think I'll stay here, where it's safe, near my nest,
Because knitting," she whispered, "is what I do best!"

And so her small needles whizzed clickety-clack,

Until clickety . . .

"CLUCK!"

Mavis froze . . .

What was THAT?!

A flap . . .
then a flutter . . .
and in something flew!

"OH!" Mavis gasped in relief,

"Marge . . . it's YOU!"

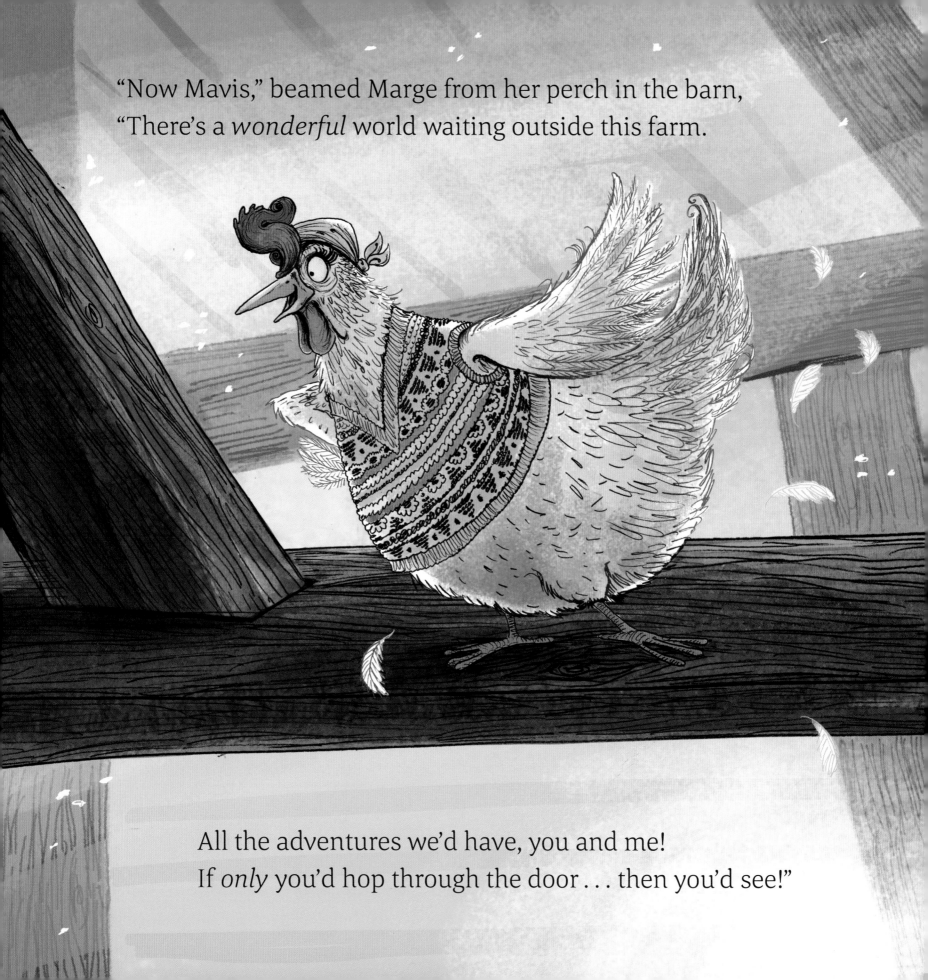

"Now Mavis," beamed Marge from her perch in the barn,
"There's a *wonderful* world waiting outside this farm.

All the adventures we'd have, you and me!
If *only* you'd hop through the door . . . then you'd see!"

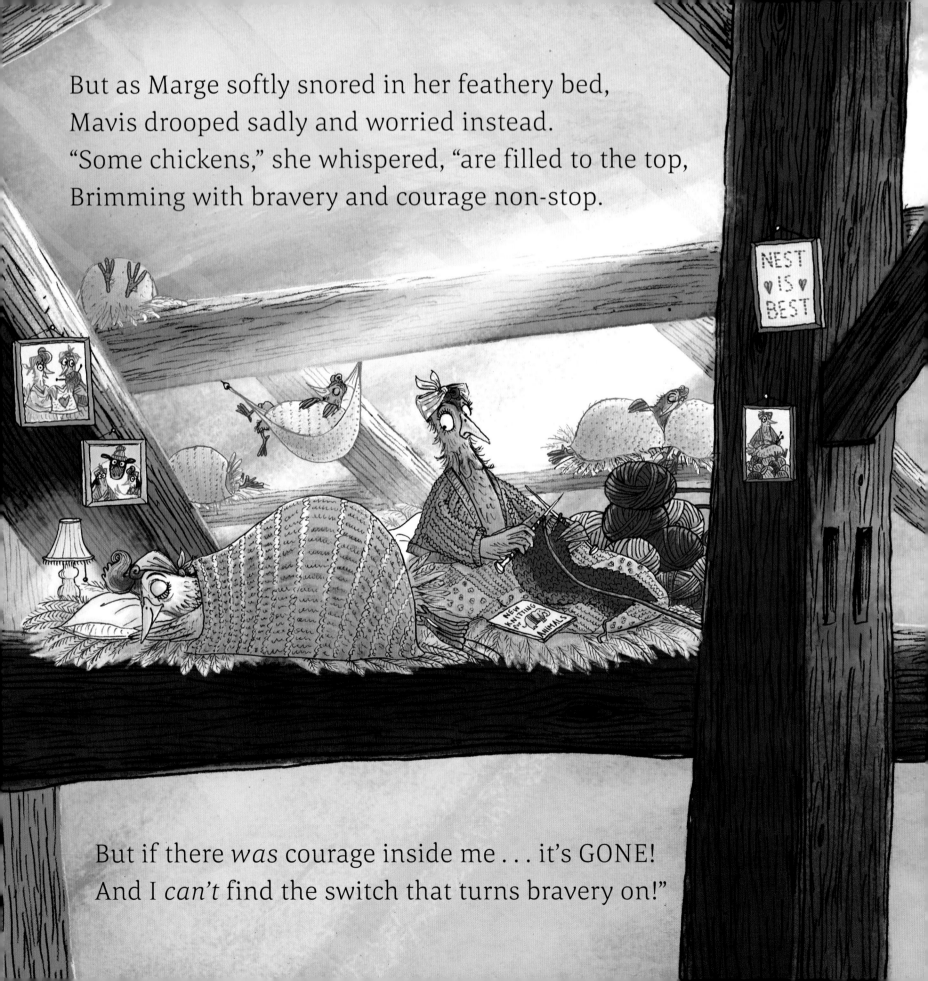

But as Marge softly snored in her feathery bed,
Mavis drooped sadly and worried instead.
"Some chickens," she whispered, "are filled to the top,
Brimming with bravery and courage non-stop.

But if there *was* courage inside me . . . it's GONE!
And I *can't* find the switch that turns bravery on!"

And once more her needles whizzed clickety-clack,
Until clickety . . .

"BAAAAA!"

Mavis froze . . .

"What was THAT?!"

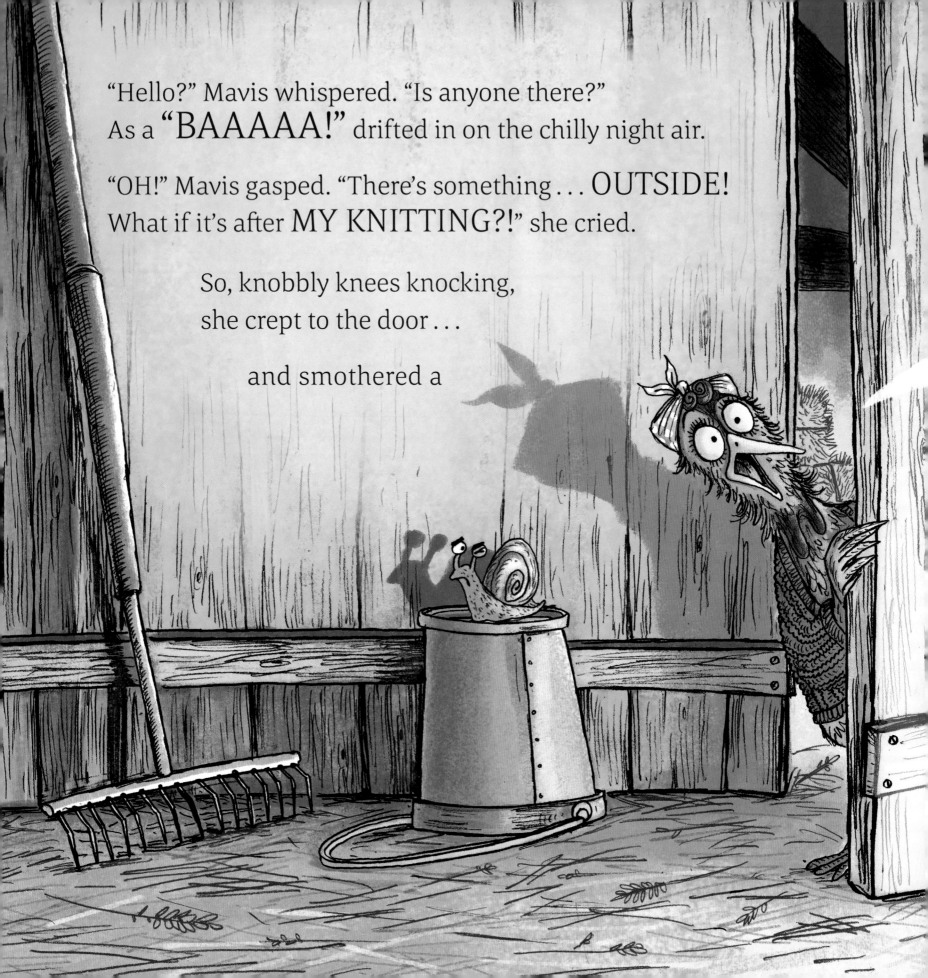

"Hello?" Mavis whispered. "Is anyone there?"
As a "BAAAAA!" drifted in on the chilly night air.

"OH!" Mavis gasped. "There's something ... OUTSIDE!
What if it's after MY KNITTING?!" she cried.

So, knobbly knees knocking,
she crept to the door ...

and smothered a

at the sight that she saw!

"MARGE!" Mavis shrieked,

"THIS IS NO TIME
TO SLEEP!

There's a THIEF on our farm
STEALING SANDRA THE SHEEP!"

"Don't panic!" cried Marge, taking off in a flurry.
"I'll fetch the farmer! Guard Sandra! Don't WORRY!"

"Don't leave me," wailed Mavis, "up here! On my own!
Just me and the thief and my scaredness . . . ALONE!"

"Oh, Mavis," clucked Marge, "look again and you'll see . . .
You *CAN* be as brave as you *WISH* you could be!"

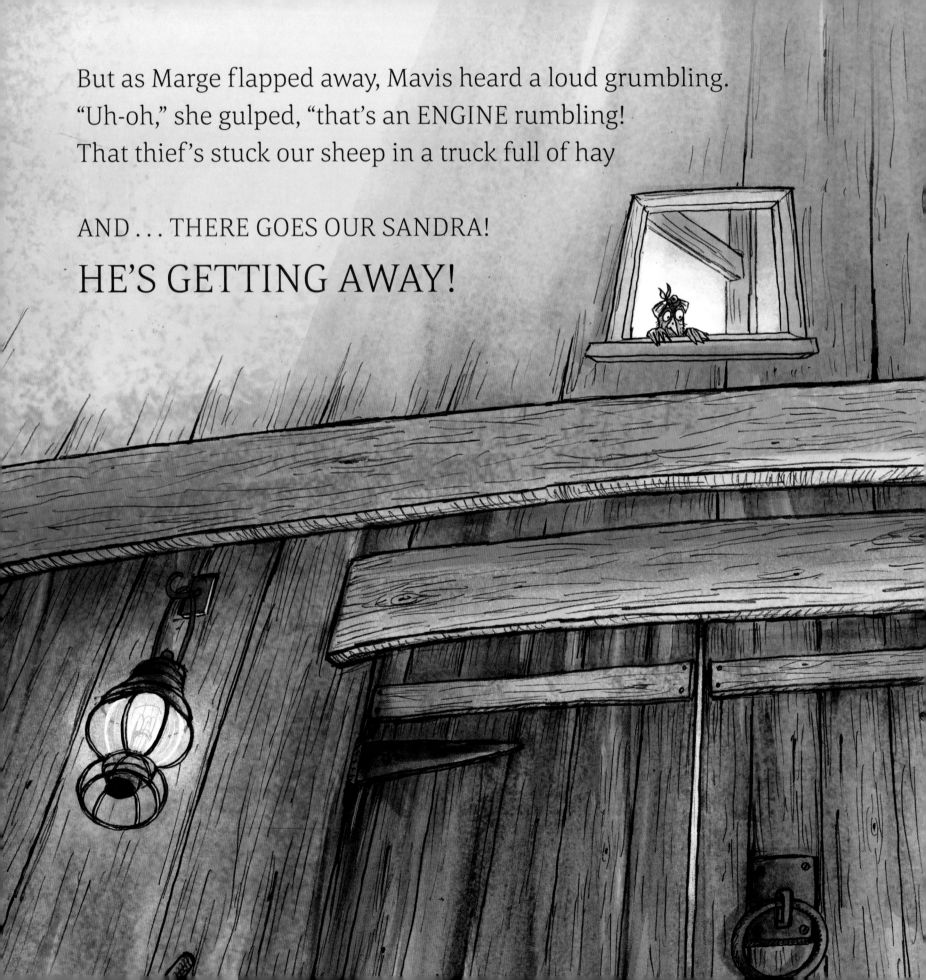

But as Marge flapped away, Mavis heard a loud grumbling.
"Uh-oh," she gulped, "that's an ENGINE rumbling!
That thief's stuck our sheep in a truck full of hay

AND . . . THERE GOES OUR SANDRA!

HE'S GETTING AWAY!

Oh, I have to do SOMETHING! Our sheep's being robbed!
I'll lose my friend AND my wool!" Mavis sobbed.

"Oh, please," she whispered, "for once, could there be
Just enough brave to save Sandra . . . in ME!"

SPEEDIES
GETAWAY VEHICLES

So she closed her eyes tightly and looked deep inside
To check all the places her braveness might hide,

And just when she thought it was darker than dark . . .

… A flicker of courage appeared like a spark!

So she took a deep breath and she dived to the floor,
"I CAN save our sheep!"
and she charged through the door!

Into the tractor next!

Goggles on face!

And **BRMMMMM!** She was off
on a wheel-spinning chase!

Mavis RUSHED through the meadow!

She RACED through the field!

She ROARED up the hill
'til her tractor tyres squealed!

"Oh!" Mavis cried. "I know *just* what to do!"
CLICK-CLACK! went her needles . . .

. . . "TA-DAAAA!

A LASSO!"

Then twirling and whirling,
she threw the rope high . . .

. . . 'Til it twanged round the thief
and she pinged through the sky!

"CLUCCCCCKKKKAA

Mavis shrieked as she rocketed up . . .

… Then she rocketed down and went PLOP! in the truck!

"AAAAARRRGGGH!" roared the sheep thief.

"TAKE THAT!" Mavis said,
As she pecked the thief hard
on the top of his head!

WHOOOMPH through the hedge!

SPLASH through the stream!

Then they SCREECHED to a halt in a great cloud of steam.

The farmer came running with Marge by his side.
"You're a **sheep-saving,
thief-braving** MARVEL!" they cried.

"BAAAAA!" agreed Sandra, and Mavis
blushed brightly.

"Our BRAVEST of hens!" Marge said,
hugging her tightly.

And there, in the star-dusted field, Mavis knew
That wherever you go and whatever you do,
When you need it the most, when you're scared or faint-hearted,
You CAN find the switch that gets bravery started . . .

For, no matter how fearful,
or feathery, or small,

There's a bright spark of braveness...

...inside us ALL!